Ant Plays Bear

A Viking Easy-to-Read

by Betsy Byars

illustrations by Marc Simont

VIKING

VIKING
Published by the Penguin Group
Penguin Books USA Inc., 375 Hudson Street, New York, New York 10014, U.S.A.
Penguin Books Ltd, 27 Wrights Lane, London W8 5TZ, England
Penguin Books Australia Ltd, Ringwood, Victoria, Australia
Penguin Books Canada Ltd, 10 Alcorn Avenue, Toronto, Ontario, Canada M4V 3B2
Penguin Books (N.Z.) Ltd, 182-190 Wairau Road, Auckland 10, New Zealand

Penguin Books Ltd, Registered Offices: Harmondsworth, Middlesex, England

First published in 1997 by Viking, a division of Penguin Books USA Inc.

7   9   10   8   6

LIBRARY OF CONGRESS CATALOGING-IN-PUBLICATION DATA
Byars, Betsy Cromer.
Ant plays Bear / by Betsy Byars; illustrations by Marc Simont.
p.   cm. — (A Viking easy-to-read)
Summary: Ant and his brother play a game, discuss growing up,
hear a scary noise, and learn to be friends.
ISBN 0-670-86776-4 (hc)
[1. Brothers—Fiction.] I. Simont, Marc, ill. II. Title. III. Series.
PZ7.B9836Ant 1997
[E]—dc21 96-48278 CIP AC

Viking® and Easy-to-Read® are registered trademarks of Penguin Books USA Inc.

Printed in Singapore
Set in Bookman

Reading Level 1.5

ANT PLAYS BEAR

"**L**et's play..."

Anthony said slowly.

He stopped to think.

He started again.

"Let's play..."

He stopped to think.

"Let's play..."

This time his thinking worked.

"Let's play Bear."

"Oh, I don't know," I said.

"I'm tired.

I've been raking leaves."

Ant said, "Please please please please—"

"Oh, all right," I said.

"How do you play?"

"One of us is the bear," Ant said.

"The other one is the person."

"What does the bear do?" I asked.

"Does he run around and climb trees?

Or does he lie down in a cave?

If he lies down in a cave.

I will be the bear."

"Yes!" said the Ant.

"I will make the cave."

He got a blanket.

He put it over a table.

He said, "Go inside."

I crawled in.

I lay down.

I said, "This is it?

This is the game?"

"Yes," said the Ant.

"While you are lying there,

I come along.

I am the person.

I am humming and picking flowers.

I don't know you are in there."

I waited in the cave.

I was bored.

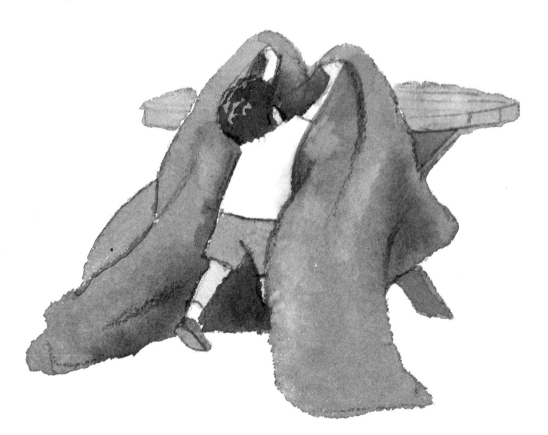

I heard Ant coming along, humming.

I went, "*Grrrrr.*"

The humming stopped.

Ant said, "I heard something.

Did you hear something?

I heard something like growls."

I went, "*Grrrrr.*"

Ant said, "Is that you growling?

It sounded like a real bear."

A real bear!

I began to like this game.

"*Grrrrrrr.*"

Ant said, "Was that you?

Did you just go *grrrrrr*?"

I went, "*Grrrrrrrr!*"

Ant said, "I'm not playing anymore.

I do not like this game."

"*Grrrrrrr!*"

Ant said, "Stop that!

I am not playing!"

He pulled off the blanket.

He looked at me.

I looked at the Ant.

I went, "*Grrrr.*"

He said, "I knew it was you.

I knew it all the time.

But let's not play Bear anymore.

All right?"

"All right," I said.

MY DOG, ANT

Ant was down on the floor.

I said, "Get up, Ant."

Ant said, "*Bow wow.*"

I said, "Are you being a dog again?"

12

"*Bow wow.*"

"Well, stop it. My new friend
is coming over.
I don't want him to think
my brother is a dog."

Ant sat up and begged.

"*Bow wow.*"

"That is not funny, Ant.
Now, stop it," I said.

I went to the window to look
for my friend.
The Ant came, too.
He sat up.

"*Bow wow.*"

I yelled, "Mom!
Ant is acting like a dog again,
and my friend is coming over.
Make him stop."

My mother came in.

She said, "What a nice dog.

I bet he wants a pat on the head."

"*Bow wow.*"

She patted him.

"And a cookie?"

"*Bow wow!*"

"Well, come on into the kitchen."

Ant started into the kitchen.

The doorbell rang.

Ant turned around.

He ran to the door.

"*Bow wow wow wow wow!*"

I opened the door.

My friend came in.

He said, "Who's that?"

I said, "My brother.

He's being a dog."

We went outside.

The Ant came, too.

My friend said,

"You know what I do

to get rid of my dog?"

I said, "What?"

He said, "I get a stick

and throw it."

He found a stick.

Ant said, "*Bow wow wow.*"

"I throw the stick—"

He got ready to throw it.

"—the dog runs after it,

and I run away and hide.

When the dog comes back,

he can't find me.

It's fun."

He looked at the Ant.

"You want a stick?

Run after the stick!"

My friend threw the stick.

Ant got up

But he did not go after the stick

He walked into the house.

He shut the door.

"Ant, come on back. Ant!"

I called.

"Let him go," my friend said.

My friend and I played for an hour,

but I did not have fun.

After he went home,

I went into the house.

The Ant was looking at a book.

I said, "Ant?"

Ant said, "That is really mean,

to throw a stick for a dog

and run away.

I am glad I am not a dog."

"I am, too, Ant."

"And if I ever have a dog,

I will never do that," said Ant.

"I won't either, Ant," I said.

"Promise?"

"I promise."

"Me, too," said the Ant.

SOMETHING AT
THE WINDOW

T

ap tap.

"There is someone tapping

on our window," Ant said.

"Ant, I am trying to get to sleep."

"Me, too, but I can't.

Someone is tapping on the window."

I said, "Ant, be real.

Our room is on the second floor.

No one could tap on our window."

"A giant could," Ant said.

"There are no giants," I said.

"Well, someone with very long legs."

"Everyone with very long legs

is playing basketball.

Now, Ant, go to sleep," I said.

"Will you look?" Ant asked.

"What?"

"Will you pull back the curtain and look?"

"Then will you go to sleep?" I said.

"Yes," said Ant.

I went to the window.

I pulled back the curtain

"There is nobody there," I said.

"Then what is going *tap tap*

like that?"

"The tree. The tree!" I said.

"The wind is blowing.

A branch of the tree is tapping

at the window."

I got back into bed.

"Good night, Ant."

"See, I was right," Ant said.

"There was somebody

tapping on the window."

"A tree! A tree!" I said.

"A tree is not somebody!

"Now this is the last time
I'm saying this.
Good night, Ant!"
"Good night."
Then Ant said softly,
"Good night, tree."
Tap tap.

WHEN ANT
GROWS UP

"I know what I am going to be when I grow up," Ant said.

"What?" I said.

"Guess."

I thought about it.

I said, "A fireman."

"And ride on fire trucks?" Ant asked.

"And put out fires?"

"Yes," I said.

You have to guess," said Ant.

I said, "Give me a hint."

Ant thought about it.

He said, "Here is the hint.

I am going to be the same as Dad."

"You're going to be

a teacher, Ant?" I said.

He said, "No!

Not a teacher!

I am going to be a man.

And after I get to be a man,

then maybe I will be a fireman,

or a farmer,

or a doctor,

or a teacher."

"Good thinking," I said.

He said, "What are you going to be?"

I said, "The same thing—a man."

He said, "We're going to be the
same thing!

"We're going to be
the exact same thing.
Mom and Dad have to hear this!"

"Ant," I said,
"it can wait until we get home.
Trust me.
It can wait."

"Oh, all right," said Ant,
"but I want to be the one
to tell them."

"You will be, Ant," I said.
"You will."